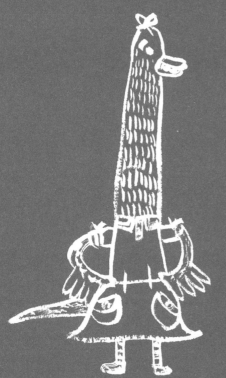

WITHDRAWN

STYGIMOLOCH: stig-uh-MOE-lock

GALLIMIMUS: gal-uh-MY-mus

PTERANODON: tuh-RAN-uh-don

TRICERATOPS: try-SAIR-uh-tops

IGUANODON: ig-GWAN-uh-don

TYRANNOSAURUS WRECKS!

by SUDIPTA BARDHAN-QUALLEN

illustrated by ZACHARIAH OHORA

ABRAMS BOOKS FOR YOUNG READERS
NEW YORK

Apatosaurus colors.

Pteranodon inspects.

Velociraptor glitters.

TYRANNOSAURUS...

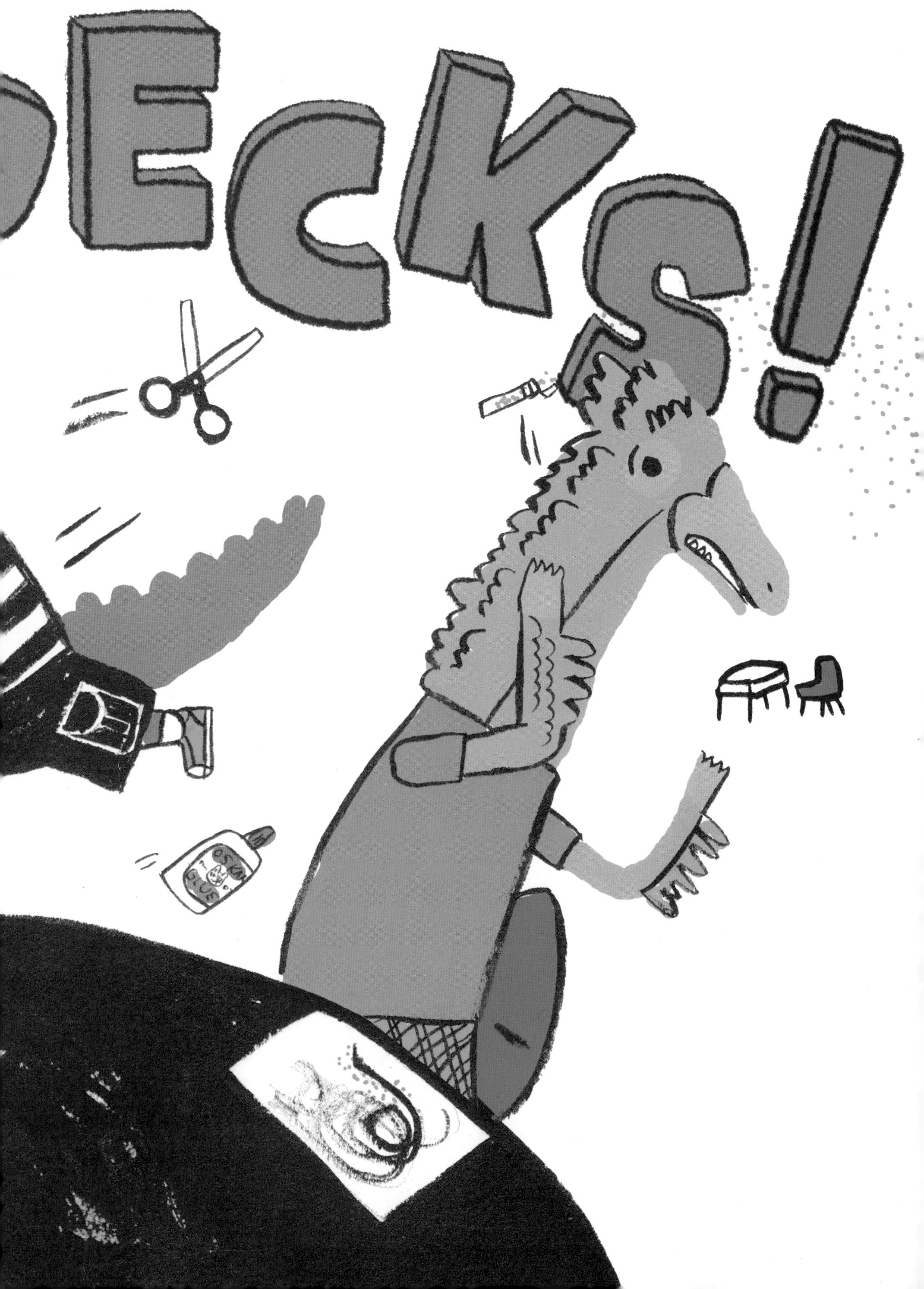
ECKS!

Triceratops erects.

Stegosaurus stacks.

Gallimimus builds it up.

TYRANNOSAURUS...

Styracosaurus copies.

Stygimoloch checks.

Iguanodon picks out a book.

TYRANNOSAURUS...

"Tyrannosaurus—knock it off!"

"Tyrannosaurus—go!"

Tyrannosaurus leaving—
Dinosaurs are glad.

Tyrannosaurus lonely,
Miserable, and sad.

Tyrannosaurus fixes,
Erases, and corrects.

Tyrannosaurus tidies, but

TYRANNOSAURUS...

Tyrannosaurus crying
Giant dino tears.
Tyrannosaurus giving up . . .

When dinos say, "Come here!"

Tyrannosaurus colors,
Pteranodon directs.

Tyrannosaurus builds and stacks,
Triceratops protects.

Tyrannosaurus careful—
Checks and double-checks.

Tyrannosaurus grateful . . . then . . .

APATOSAURUS WREC

IN HONOR OF SAWYERSAURUS REX,
DISCOVERED ON OCTOBER 20, 2006
—S.B.Q.

FOR LYDIA, OSKAROSAURUS
& TEDDY REX
—Z.O.

The illustrations in this book were made with
with Sumi ink and brush on Arches watercolor
paper, with color added digitally.

Library of Congress Cataloging-in-Publication Data

Bardhan-Quallen, Sudipta.
Tyrannosaurus wrecks! / by Sudipta Bardhan-Quallen ;
illustrated by Zachariah OHora.
pages cm
Summary: "All the dinosaurs play nicely, except
Tyrannosaurus wrecks"— Provided by publisher.
ISBN 978-1-4197-1035-3
[1. Stories in rhyme. 2. Tyrannosaurus rex—Fiction.
3. Dinosaurs—Fiction. 4. Behavior—Fiction.]
I. OHora, Zachariah, illustrator. II. Title.
PZ8.3.B237Ty 2014
[E]—dc23
2013022197

Printed and bound in China
10 9 8 7 6 5 4 3 2

Abrams Books for Young Readers are available at special discounts
when purchased in quantity for premiums and promotions as well
as fundraising or educational use. Special editions can also be created
to specification. For details, contact specialsales@abramsbooks.com
or the address below.

THE ART OF BOOKS SINCE 1949
115 West 18th Street
New York, NY 10011
www.abramsbooks.com

VELOCIRAPTOR: vuh-LOS-ih-RAP-tor

STYRACOSAURUS: stih-RACK-uh-SAWR-us

TYRANNOSAURUS: tie-RAN-uh-SAWR-us

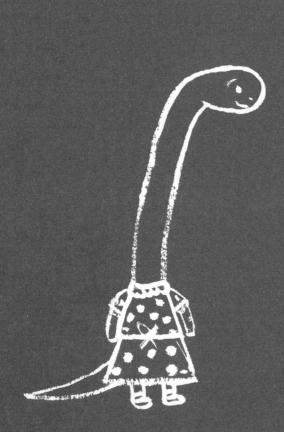

APATOSAURUS: ah-PAT-uh-SAWR-us

STEGOSAURUS: steg-uh-SAWR-us